The Bir

by Linda Koons • illustrated by S. Laberis

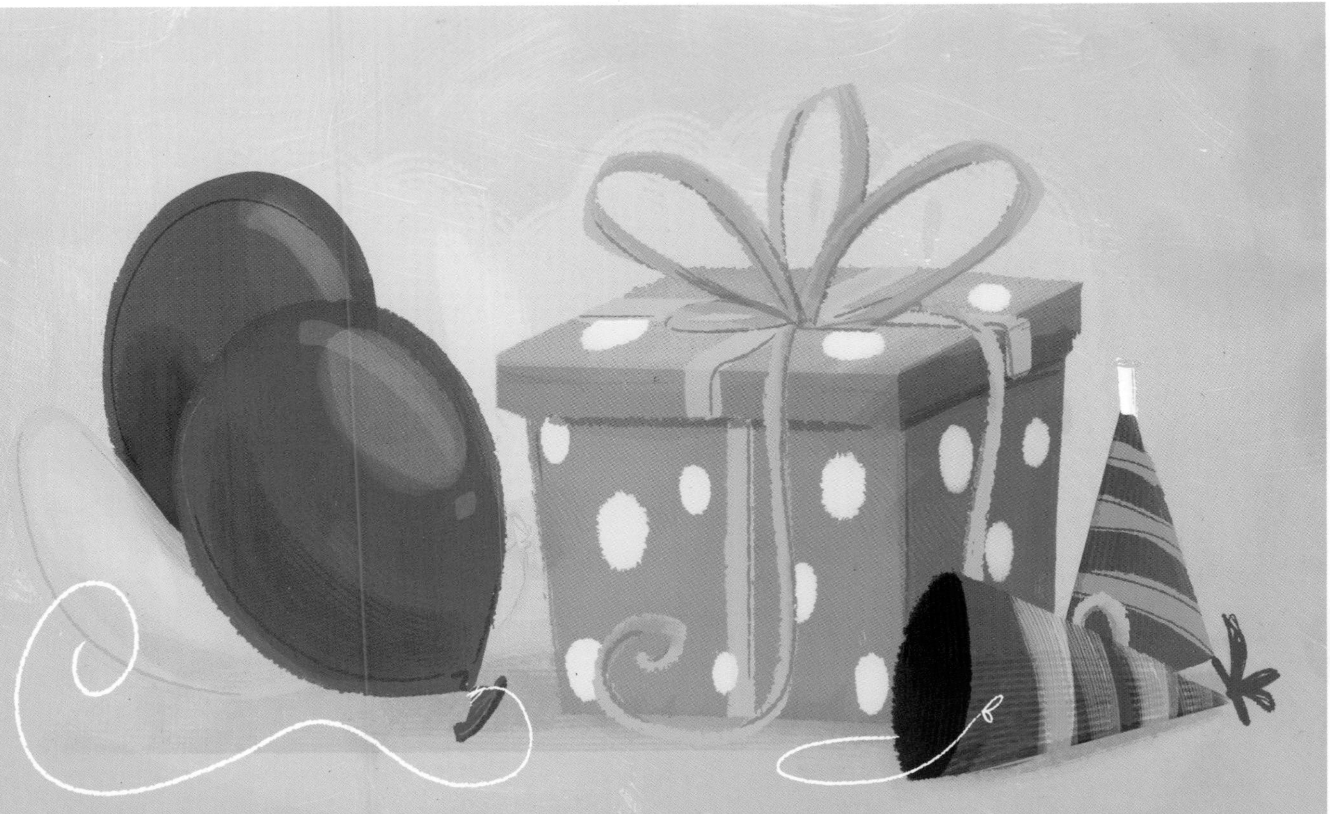

It is a balloon.

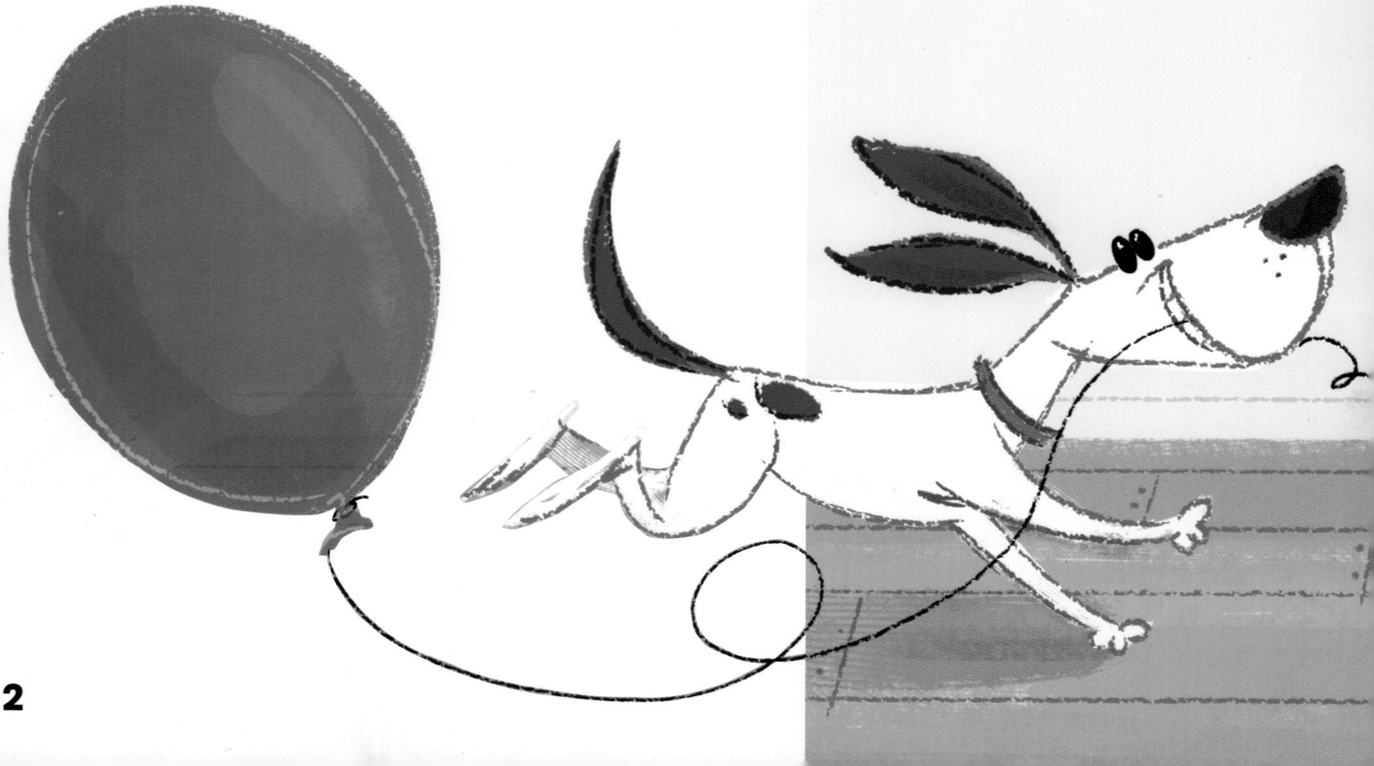

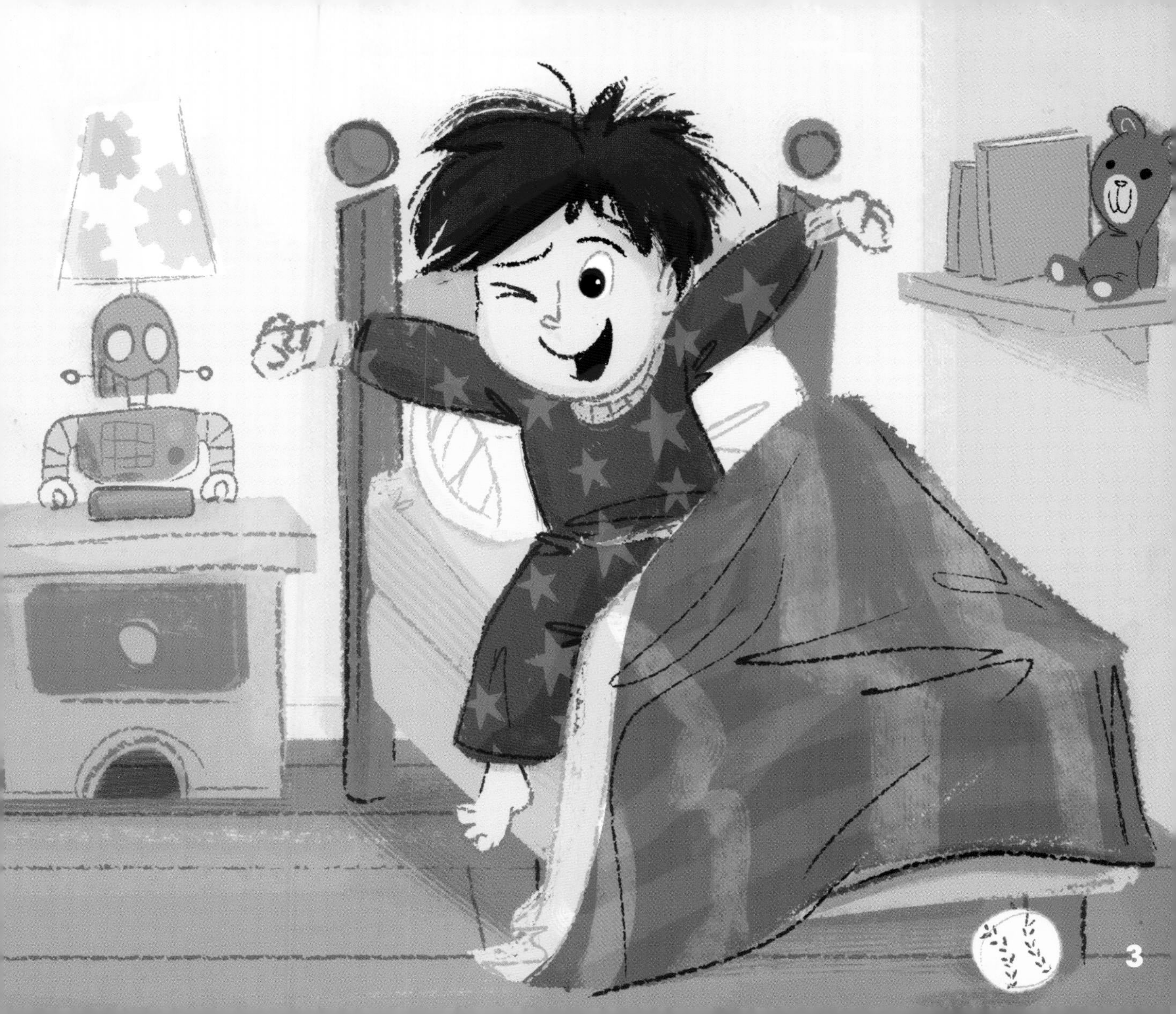

It is a candle.

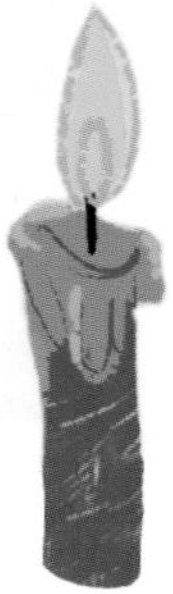

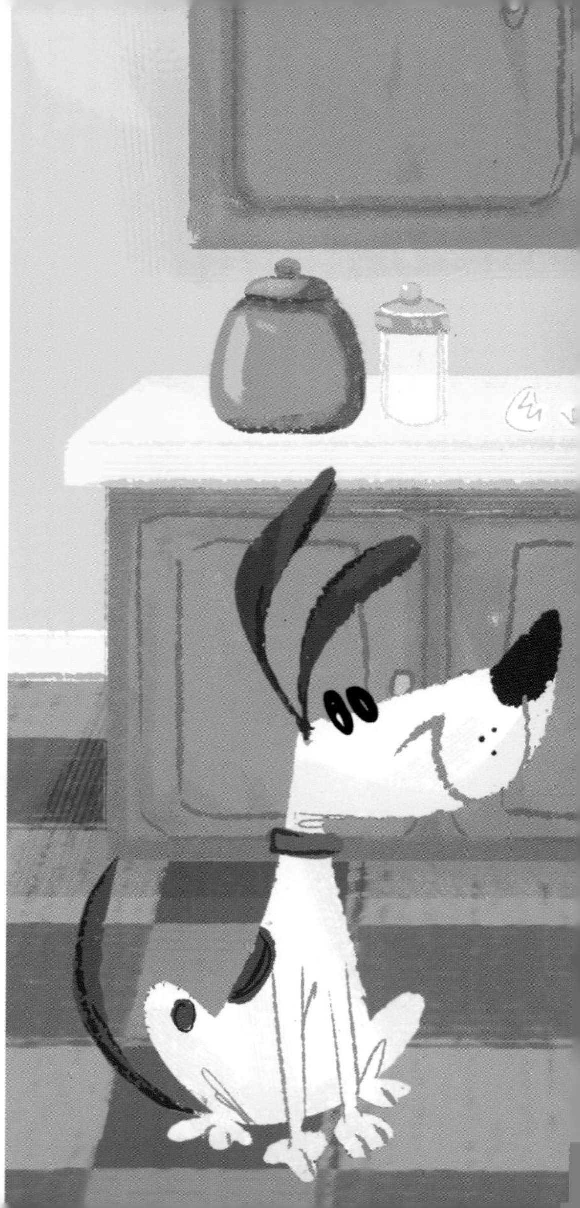

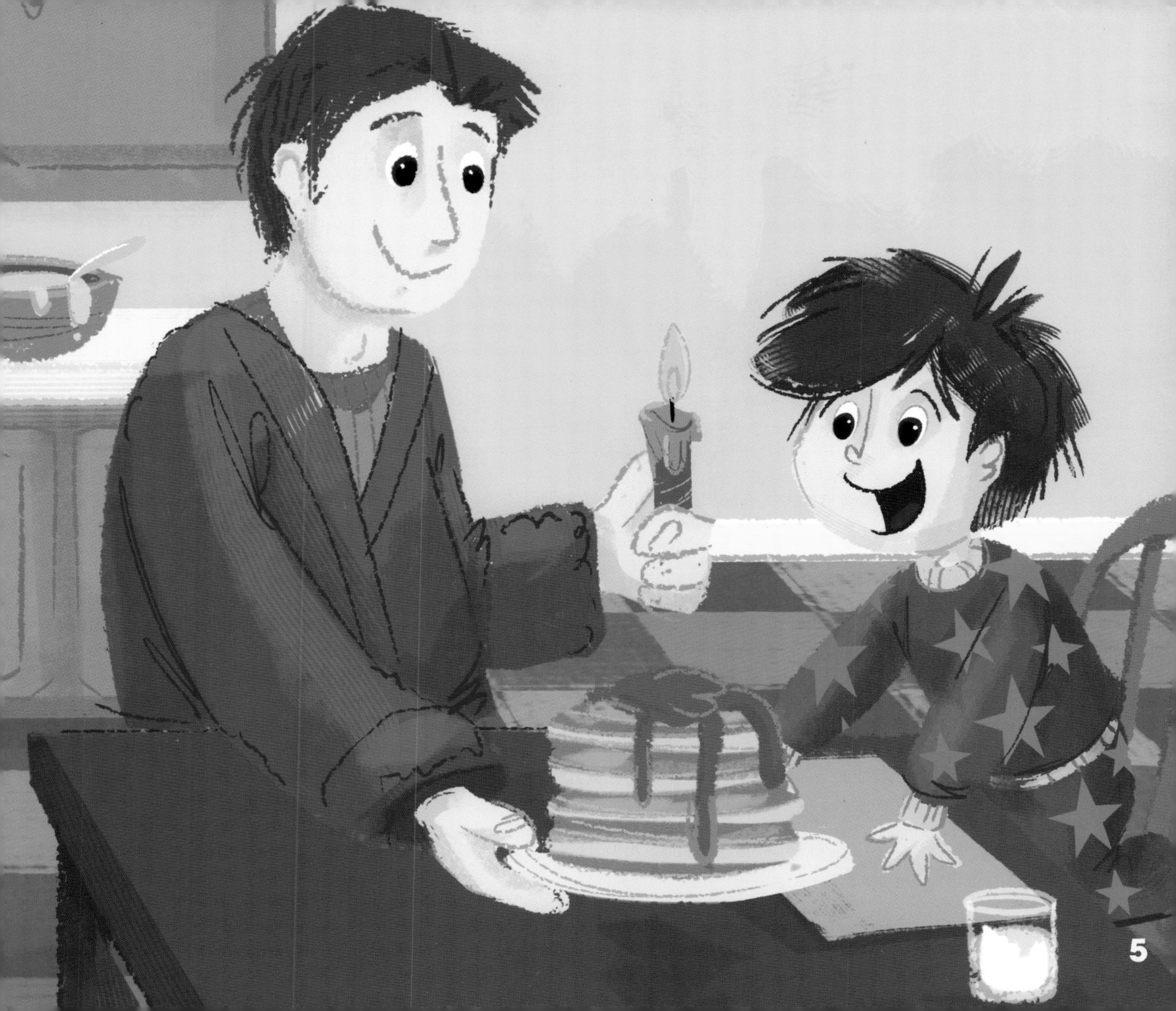

It is a horn.

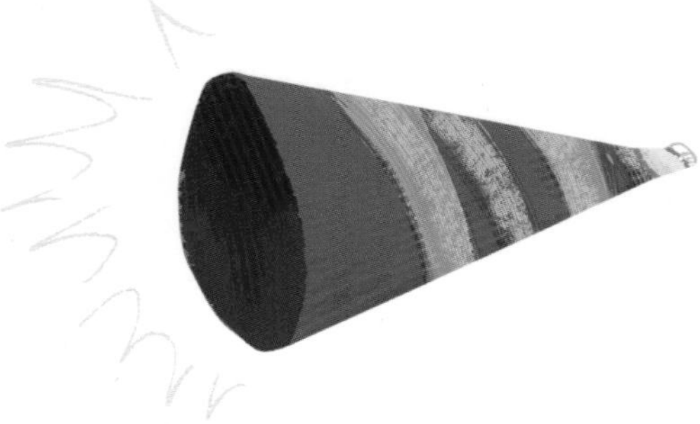

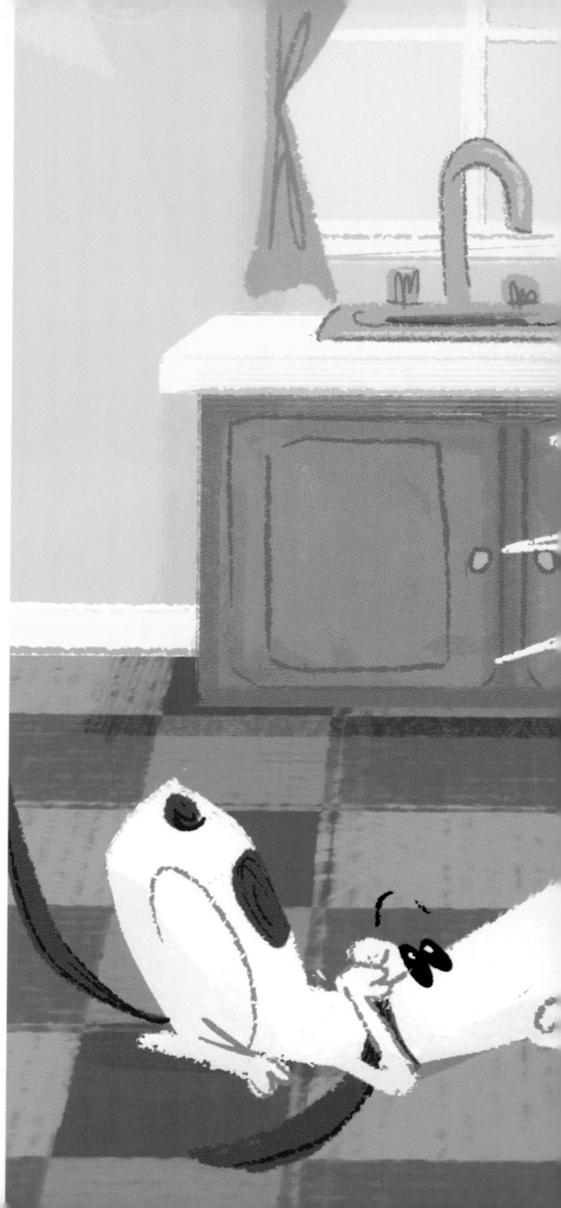

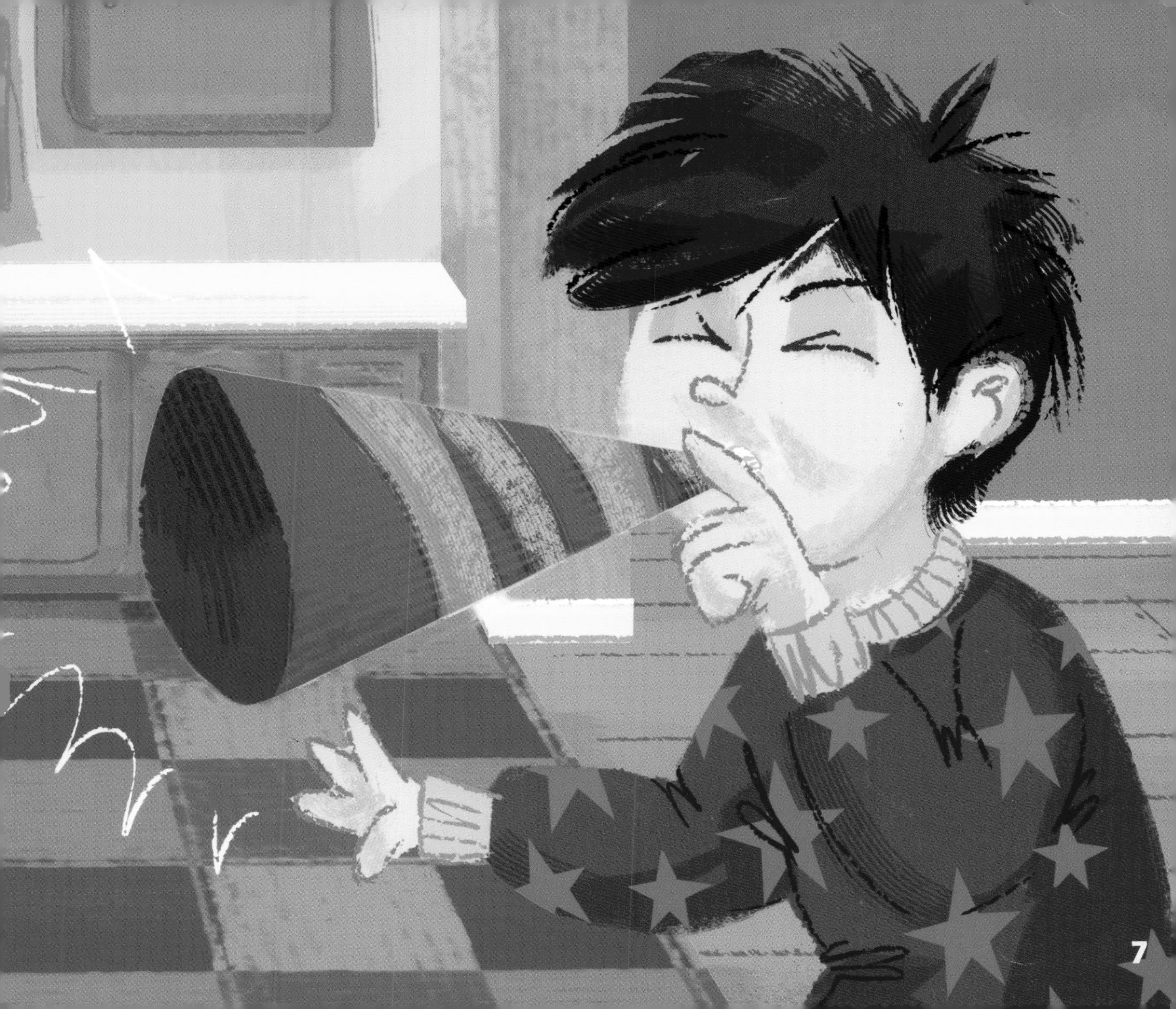

It is a bow.

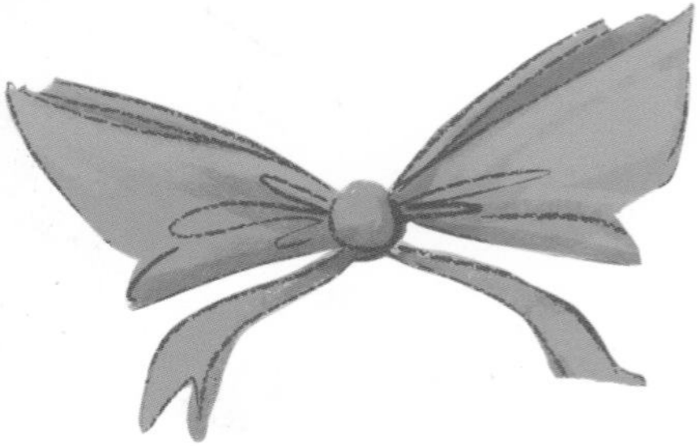

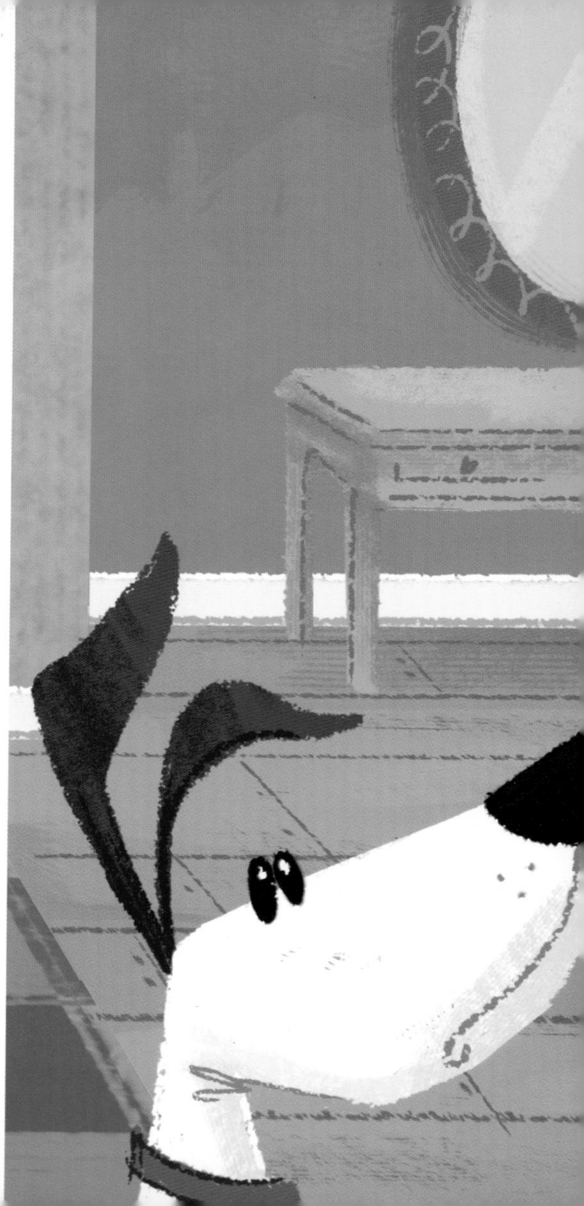

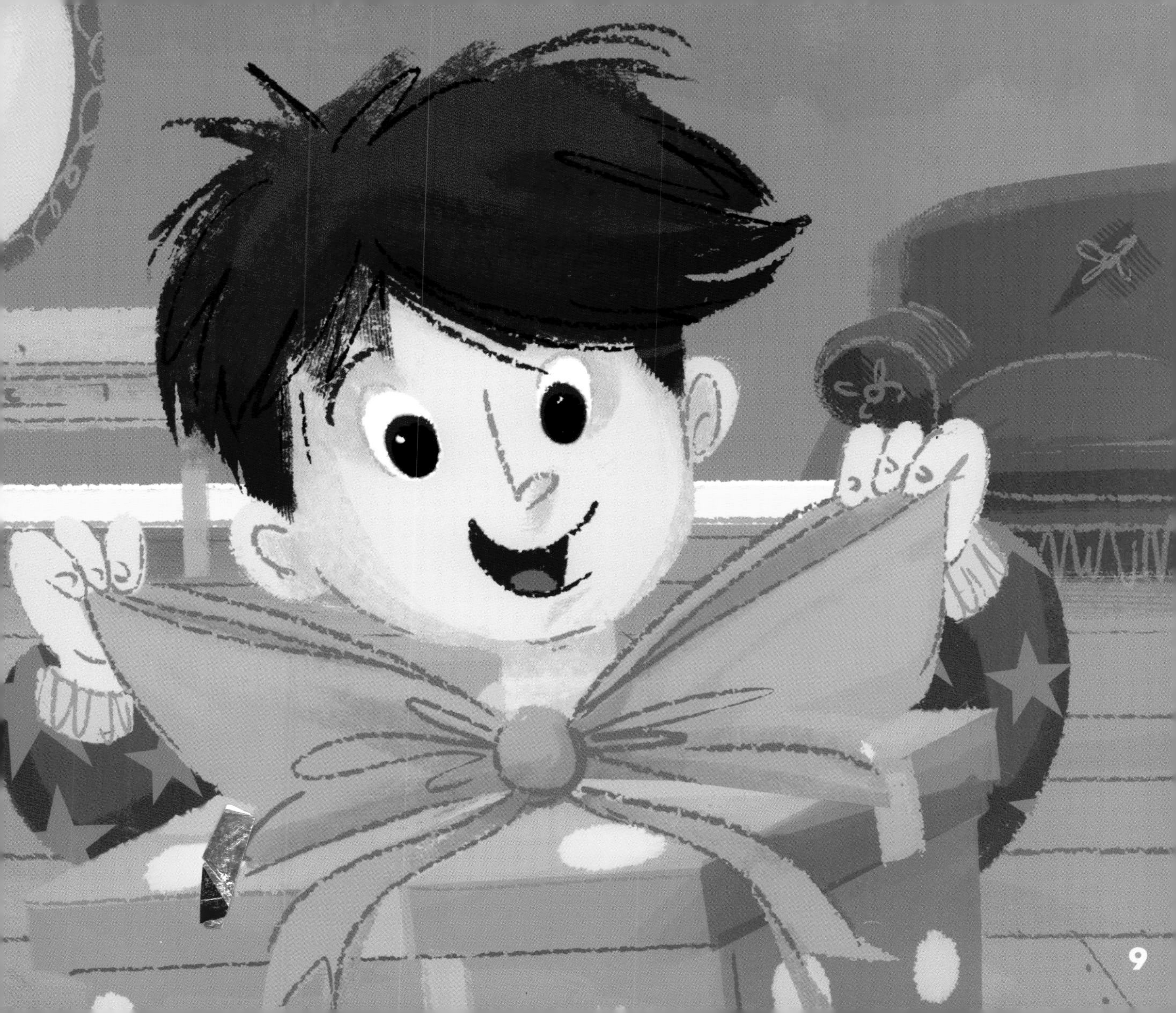

It is a box.

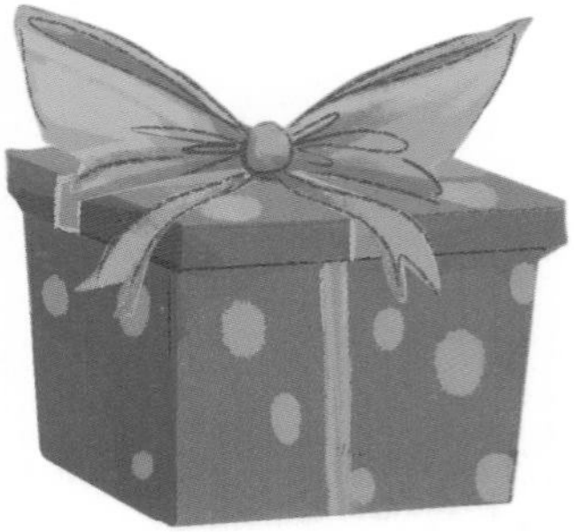

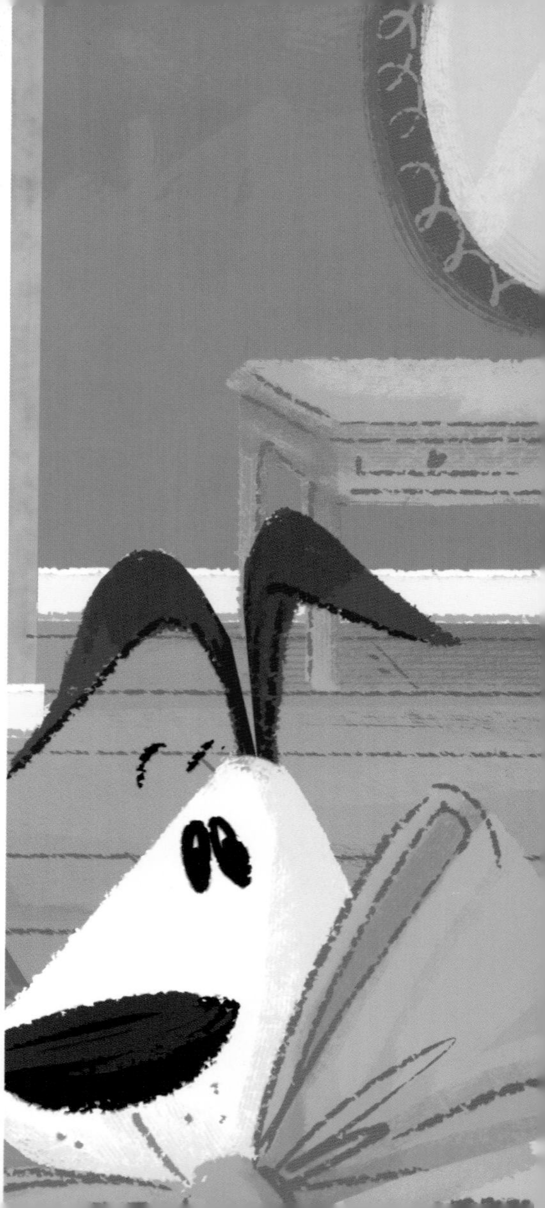

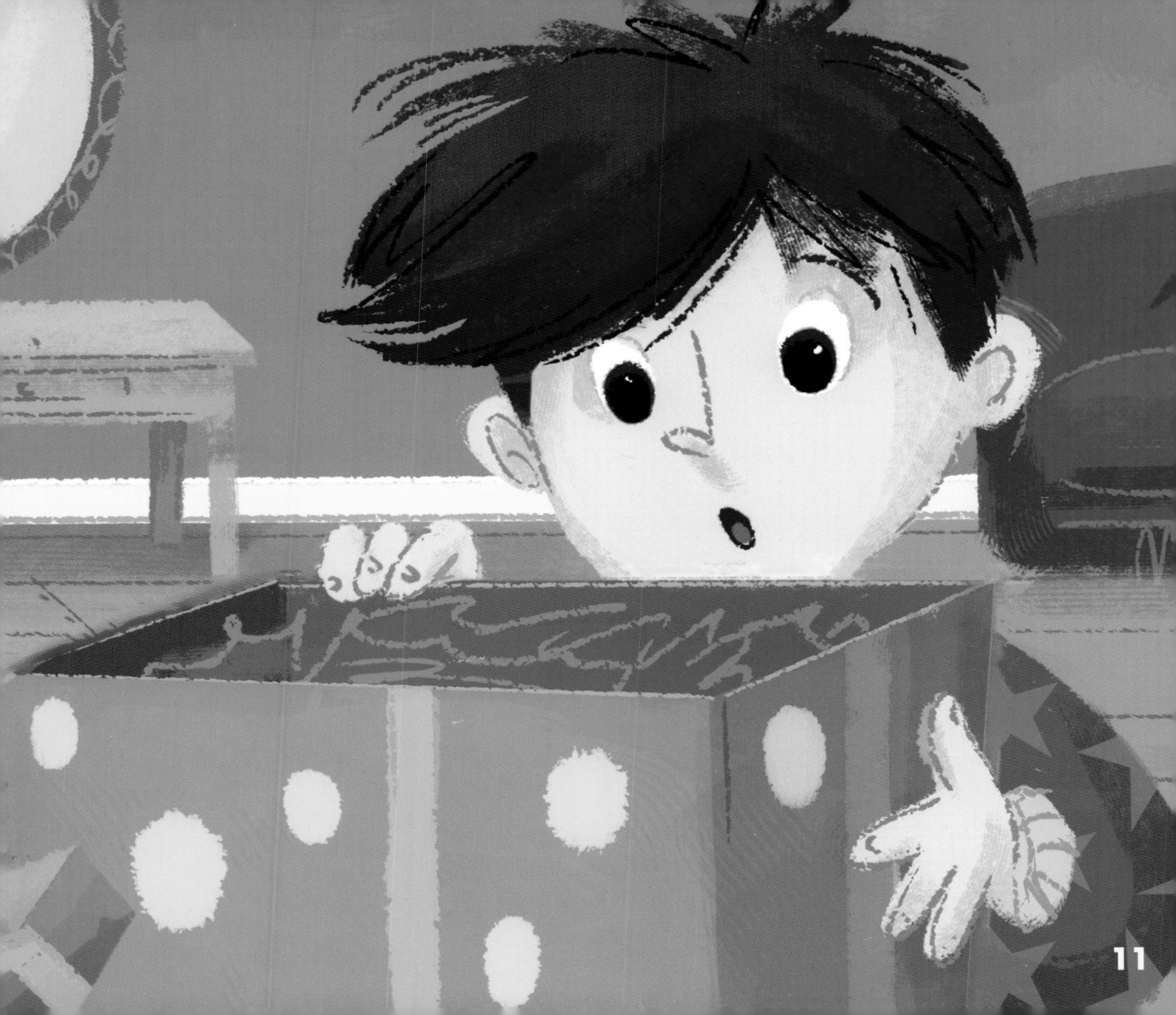

It is a boat.

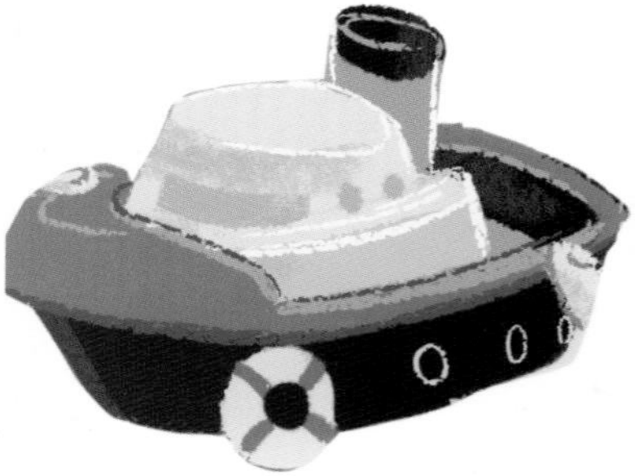

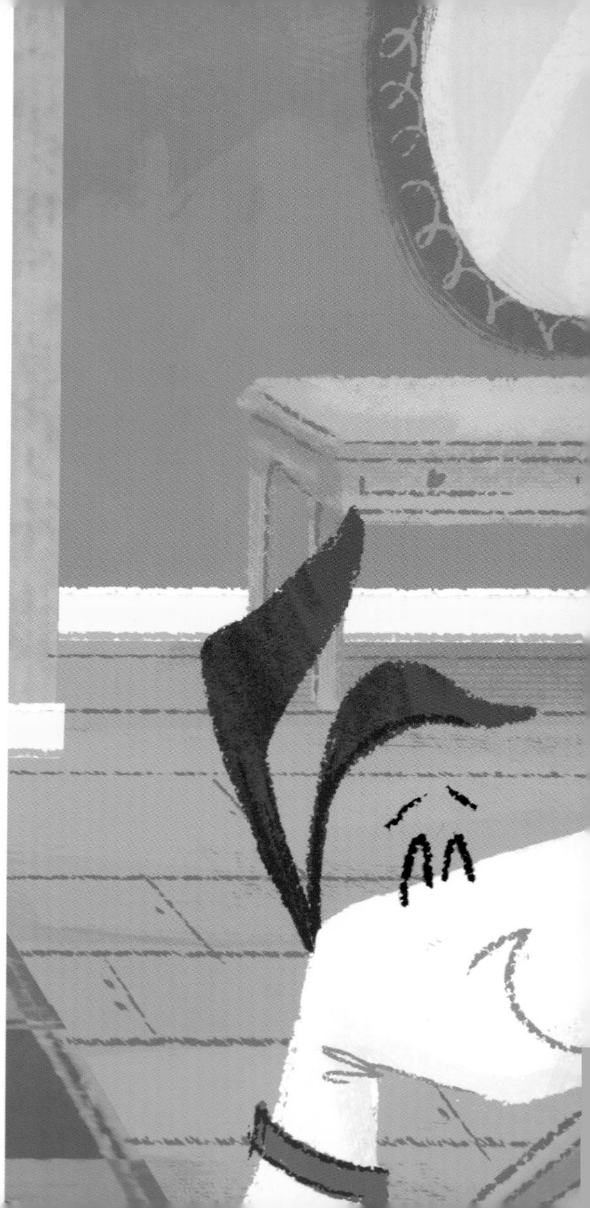

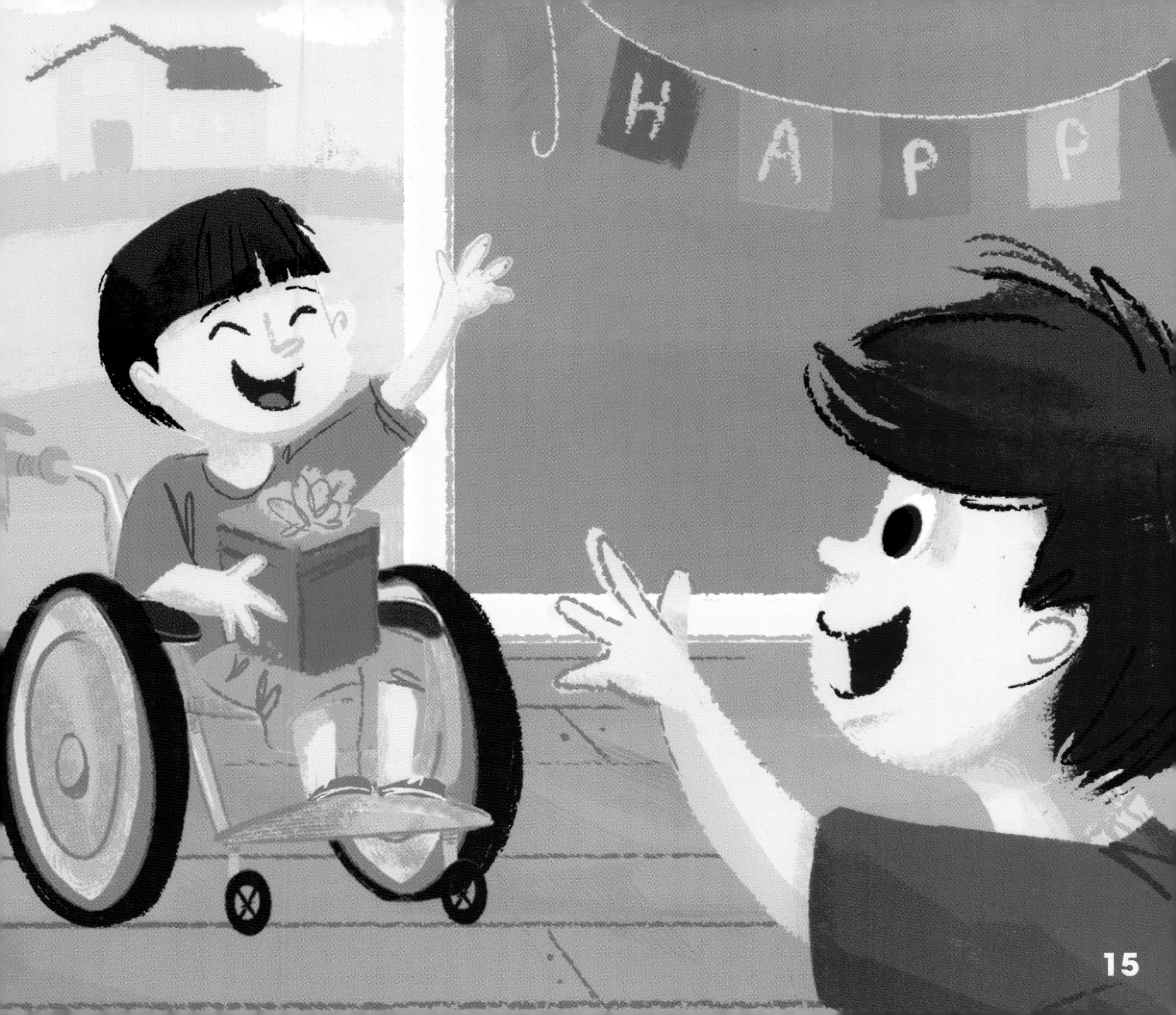
HAPP

It is a party!

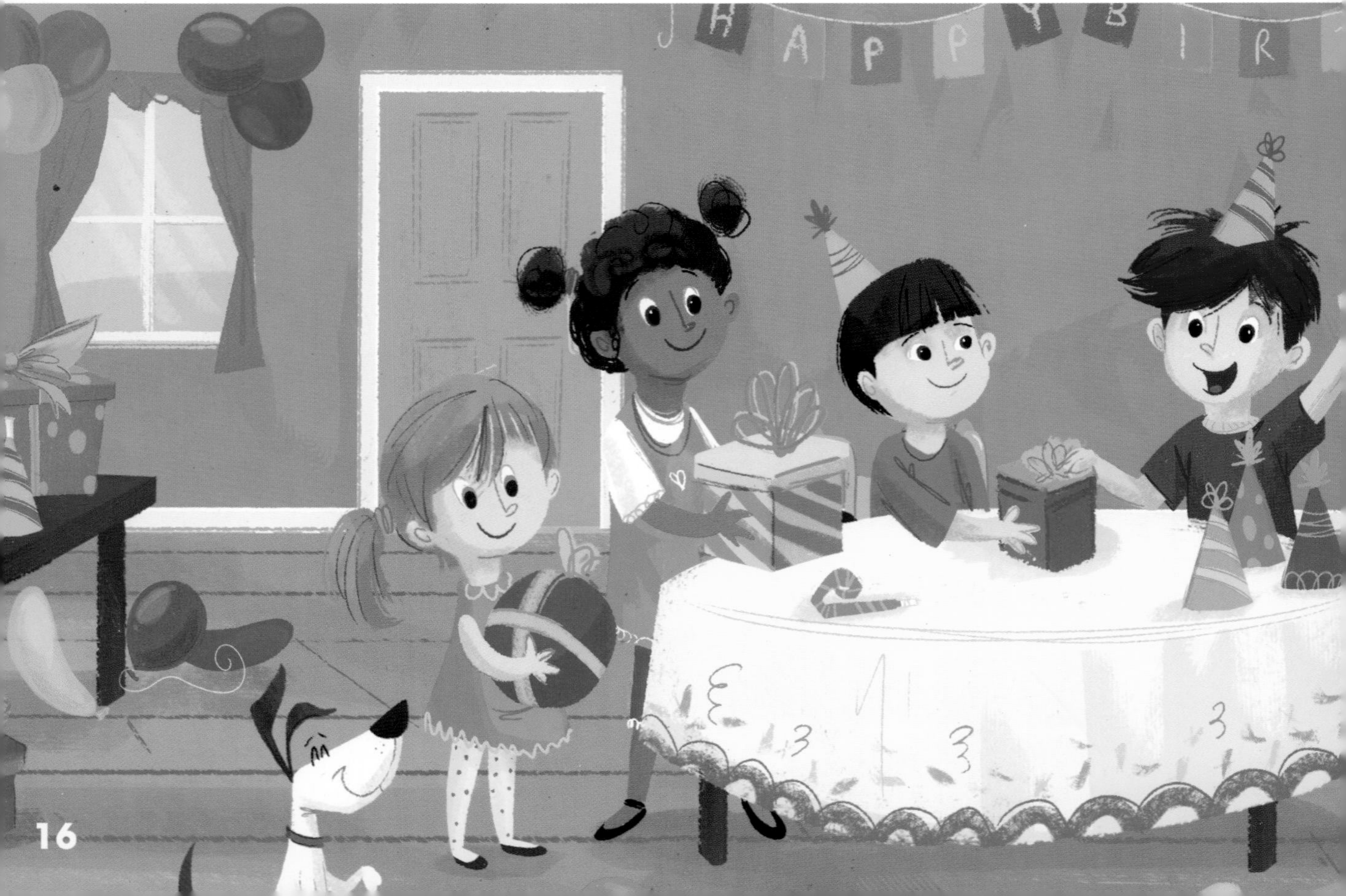